3.99

Busytown Mysteries™

With the timeless characters of RICHARD SCARRY

Mr. Fixit's Lucky Day

adapted by Natalie Shaw
based on the screenplay
"The Mystery of the Missing Pirate Gold"
written by Pete Sauder

with illustrations
by Susan Hall

Simon Spotlight
New York   London   Toronto   Sydney

SIMON SPOTLIGHT

An imprint of Simon & Schuster Children's Publishing Division

1230 Avenue of the Americas, New York, New York 10020

Busytown Mysteries™ and all related and associated trademarks are owned by Cookie Jar Entertainment Inc. and used under license from Cookie Jar Entertainment Inc. © 2011 Cookie Jar Entertainment Inc. All rights reserved. All rights reserved, including the right of reproduction in whole or in part in any form.

SIMON SPOTLIGHT and colophon are registered trademarks of Simon & Schuster, Inc.

For information about special discounts for bulk purchases, please contact Simon & Schuster Special Sales at 1-866-506-1949 or business@simonandschuster.com.

Manufactured in the United States of America 0411 LAK

First Edition 10 9 8 7 6 5 4 3 2 1

ISBN 978-1-4424-2085-4

It was a perfect day in Busytown. The sun was shining, the sky was blue, and there was a cool breeze in the air.

"Great idea to come to the Busytown Beach, Huckle!" said Sally.

They looked out at the beach. It seemed like everyone in Busytown had the same idea. It was really crowded!

All of a sudden there was a beeping sound.
It was coming from Mr. Fixit's metal detector.

"I'll bet that beeping means he found
something!" said Sally.

Huckle, Sally, and Lowly rushed over to Mr. Fixit just as he dug something out of the sand. It was a gold coin!

"Yahoo! I'm going to be rich!" shouted Mr. Fixit. "That makes twenty gold pirate coins I've found today. But don't tell anyone . . . it's a secret!"

Oops, it was too late! *Everyone* had heard Mr. Fixit.

Within moments everyone started digging with anything they could find: shovels, clam shells, and even swim masks.

And as soon as Mr. Fixit put the coin in his bag, his metal detector started beeping again.

"Another one! This makes twenty-one pirate coins," Mr. Fixit shouted, as he picked up an identical gold coin from the sand at his feet.

"This sure is your lucky day!" said Huckle.

Mr. Fixit was about to put the coin in his bag, when he noticed it felt light. *Too light*. He asked Huckle to hold the coin while he turned his bag upside down. Nothing fell out!

"Oh, no!" cried Mr. Fixit. "My bag is empty! All of the coins are gone."

"But that's impossible," said Sally. "We saw you put a coin in there!"

"It looks to me like we have a *mystery*!" said Huckle.

Just then Goldbug rode in on a surfboard to get the news scoop.

"So what's making a big splash at the beach, Huckle?" asked Goldbug.

"Well, Goldbug," answered Huckle. "Mr. Fixit's gold coins are missing! We have to find them!"

"That's the word on the beach," said Goldbug. "Stay tuned for important news updates!"

Suddenly they heard Pig Will and Pig Won't yelling from above. They were parasailing!

"Wait a second!" said Pig Will. "If we're both up here, who's driving the boat?"

Luckily the boat slowed down, and the pigs glided down to the beach safely.

"Didn't you see that I was up there?" asked Pig Will.

"I didn't look," said Pig Won't, "because it was *your* turn to drive!"

Huckle, Sally, and Lowly sat down to think. Lowly had an idea!
"Maybe someone took Mr. Fixit's coins when he wasn't looking!" he sai
"But Mr. Fixit would have heard something," said Sally.

"Not with those big headphones on," replied Huckle.
"Hmmm. Maybe there are clues on the beach. What can we
look for in the sand?"

"Let's look for footprints!" cried Sally.

"Good work, team. Let's go!" said Huckle.

They returned to the spot where Mr. Fixit lost his coins. There were lots of different footprints in the sand.

"First let's figure out which footprints are ours," said Huckle, looking around. "These are mine!"

"And here are mine," said Sally.

"The single footprints
are mine!" said Lowly.
"And the only other
footprints here look like
they belong to Mr. Fixit."

"That means whoever
took the coins didn't leave
any footprints?" asked Sally.
"That's impossible!"

They headed to the refreshment stand to get pink lemonade and talk about the mystery.

"No one left any footprints," said Sally. "So is it possible that no one took the coins at all?"

"But if no one took them, what happened to them?" asked Lowly.

Before anyone could answer, they heard Pig Will and Pig Won't arguing again, this time about which milk shake to get.

"I want a *banana* milk shake," yelled Pig Won't, holding out a coin. "And that's what we're getting because *I* have the money."

Pig Won't stuffed the coin back in his pocket to keep Pig Will from getting it, but it went straight through the pocket and fell to the ground!

"Aha!" yelled Pig Will, as he picked the coin off the ground and stuffed it in his pocket. "Now that *I* have the money, we're getting a *strawberry* milk shake!"

The coin fell through Pig Will's pocket and landed on the ground
again! When the brothers turned their pockets inside out, they
discovered that they had big holes!

"Those pockets have more holes than a piece of Swiss cheese," said
Lowly. "Are you thinking what I'm thinking?"

"Yes!" said Huckle. "I think we've solved the mystery!"

Mr. Fixit returned just as Goldbug surfed up to the refreshment stand.

"Breaking beach news! Have you solved the mystery, Huckle?" he asked.

"I think there's a hole in Mr. Fixit's bag," said Huckle. "When he found the first coin and put it in his bag, it fell out of the hole. Then he picked up the *same* coin from the sand, thinking it was another coin and another coin, when there was actually only *one* coin."

"Sorry, Mr. Fixit. I guess this isn't your lucky day after all," said Lowly.

"Oh, I wouldn't say that, Lowly," said Mr. Fixit, holding up his gold coin. "Finding *one* gold pirate coin is a lot better than finding none! Strawberry-banana milk shakes for everyone!"

"Hurray for Huckle!" they all cheered. "Hurray for Mr. Fixit!"